Suppandi

THE LAUGHTER NEVER ENDS

A painter, a driver, a copywriter, and even a chef, Suppandi has applied his truly unique wit to almost every imaginable job out there. The perpetual optimist, Suppandi is never afraid to take up a new occupation, much to the amusement of his fans everywhere. Suppandi has remained, from the day of the character's conception, Tinkle's most popular toon.

Based on a Tamil folklore about a character called Chappandi, Suppandi was first drawn by the legendary Ram Waeerkar. His daughter, Archana Amberkar, took over after he passed away. She gave the character a more youthful look. In this collection, we have put together our favourite Suppandi stories from the last few years. In them, Suppandi has the challenge of figuring out a number of different tasks and working on a great many jobs.

Suppandi has a resume that is long enough to fill an entire book. We came up with this collection keeping that thought in mind—we do hope you love it.

Readers Speak:

"Suppandi is cool and a lovable fellow. Getting fired from jobs does not make him mellow." – **Meghna Kamath**

"Suppandi you're the best! Tinkle's iconic writers have a great sense of humour and that has made Suppandi more interesting. Suppandi is my favourite toon." – **Shivom Ghai**

"Before reading the entire comic from cover to cover, I open the magazine and read the Suppandi story first. I love Suppandi; he's my favourite Tinkle toon." – **Shivang Chawla**

"I like reading and I've been reading Tinkle since the last year. All of the characters are great but I think Suppandi is the funniest character of the lot." – **Khushi Paliwal**

"One day I was reading a Suppandi story and I started to laugh so hard that I hit my mother's table and as a consequence broke my mother's expensive makeup box." – **Tiameren Longkumer**

"Suppandi's antics always bring about a smile. In fact, Suppandi's stories were all I could understand back when I was eight years old. We even enacted a play based on his stories. Now, I'm 17 and Suppandi is still my favourite character."
– **Holyna Annie Gifta**

INDEX

4

SUPPANDI Creative Instincts

Story & Script	Pencils & Inks	Colours	Letters
Shruti Dave	Archana Amberkar	Umesh Sarode	Akshay Khadilkar

"HERE ARE THE REFERENCES OF WHAT FALANA AND DIMKA DID—."
Ultra soft, ultra smooth!
Glow Shampoo
SHAMPOO
A toothpaste so powerful, it lasts for up to 24 hours!
Chamku Toothpaste
AND SO, SUPPANDI PUT ON HIS CREATIVE HAT...
...AND CAME UP WITH—
A cement paste so powerful, it lasts for up to 24 hours!
Tarbooja Cement
Built on strength & sustainability

THE AD WENT TO THE CLIENT FOR APPROVAL AND HE CALLED BACK, WANTING TO HAVE A WORD WITH OUR NEW COPYWRITER—

SUPPANDI!!!!!!! WHAT DO YOU MEAN OUR CEMENT LASTS FOR ONLY 24 HOURS? AND **WHAT** HAVE YOU DONE TO OUR TARBOOJA MAN??!!!

SIR, OUR CEO ASKED US TO MIX THE FALANA SHAMPOO AND DIMKA TOOTHPASTE ADS!

HA. HA. GOOD GOING, SUP.

WHAT?!!! YOU'RE FIRED! HE'S FIRED! YOU'RE ALL FIRED!

LATER—

THAT WAS A FINE THING YOU DID, SUPPANDI. TARBOOJA IS REALLY ANGRY WITH OUR CEO'S GENIUS IDEA.

BUT I DIDN'T MEAN TO...

IT'S ALL RIGHT, BUDDY. IT'S TIME THE SUITS* REALIZE JUST HOW **CREATIVE** THEIR IDEAS ARE.

ANYWAY, OUR CEO'S PACIFIED THEM. NOW, THEY WANT US TO REPRINT AND RUN THEIR OLD ADS.

BRIING RIING!

*SLANG TERM USED TO REFER TO BUSINESSMEN OR CORPORATE WORKERS

suppandi clears the road

Story: Sujatha Menon

SUPPANDI
Weight Watch

Story: Carisa Rocha
Script: Rajani Thindiath
Illustrator: Archana Amberkar
Colourist: Umesh Sarode

Suppandi's Formula for a Quick Bath

Illustrator:
Archana Amberkar
Colourist: Umesh Sarode

SUPPANDI, I HAVE TO ATTEND A PARTY AND I'M LATE...

...I WANT TO HAVE A QUICK BATH...

WILL YOU FILL HOT WATER FOR ME?

AT ONCE, VIVEK!

WATER IS READY FOR YOUR BATH!

OH THANKS, SUPPANDI!

I HOPE THE WATER IS NICE AND HOT?

IT IS, IT IS! AND I'VE ADDED SOMETHING TO IT THAT'LL HELP YOU FINISH YOUR BATH IN DOUBLE-QUICK TIME!

WHAT IS THIS SECRET INGREDIENT, SUPPANDI?

SOAP!

I'VE DISSOLVED IT IN THE WATER SO THAT YOU WON'T HAVE TO WASTE TIME APPLYING IT ON YOUR BODY!!

SUPPANDI
LOOKS FOR A JOB!

Writer: Luis
Illustrator: Archana Amberkar
Colourist: Umesh Sarode

SUPPANDI
Courier

Based on a story sent by **S. M. Kulandaisami**
Script: Rajani Thindiath
Illustrator: Archana Amberkar
Colourist: Umesh Sarode

SUPPANDI, SEND THIS LETTER BY COURIER.

VERY WELL, SIR.

AT THE COURIER OFFICE —

I WANT TO COURIER THIS LETTER. HOW MUCH WOULD IT COST?

TWENTY RUPEES.

TWENTY RUPEES! THAT'S DAYLIGHT ROBBERY! WHY, THE ADDRESS IS JUST TWO LANES AWAY!

I'M SORRY, BUT THE CHARGE IS THE SAME FOR ALL LOCAL LETTERS.

WHEN WILL IT REACH?

TOMORROW.

TWENTY RUPEES AND IT WILL BE DELIVERED ONLY TOMORROW! GIVE IT BACK TO ME!!

AT SUPPANDI'S WORKPLACE —

HE'S BEEN GONE ALMOST TWO HOURS!

17

Meet The Artist

Hello readers,
While you flip your way through the pages of this
issue, we thought you might want to take a sneak peek at
the artist who has been bringing Suppandi to life all these years,
Archana Amberkar. So we sent Suppandi to go interview Archana. This is
what he came back with. We hope you enjoy the conversation and do forgive
Suppandi if he forgot to ask an important question… or two.

When did you first start drawing me?
I started drawing you in 1992. At that time I was only doing stand-alone single page
illustrations and three-panel gags. Then one day my father, Ram Waeerkar, came to me and told
me I would be taking over the art for one of *Tinkle's* most iconic characters—you, Suppandi!

What's the most fun apart about drawing stories with me in it?
Well, apart from getting to experiment with different looks for you, I also enjoy all the different
locations the writers seem to put you in. Earlier, the stories had you only in the house, but now the
locations vary from exotic to weird.

Is there anything tough about drawing me?
Drawing you, my darling Suppandi, is my toughest and my most challenging task. You never seem to
want to show your entire face to the readers, so I have to find a way to display your range of emotions
and expressions while keeping your face slightly tilted at all times.

I've grown older and I can feel it. Can you tell that I've evolved at all?
Oh, definitely. You used to walk the streets of the
villages but now, Suppandi, you get to roam the
cities of India and pit your I.Q. against some of the
best bosses around.

**Do you have any message for the readers
who are currently going through this
collection?**
All I want to tell the readers is that
'I hope you have as much fun reading
about Suppandi as I do drawing
him'.

Text: Sean D'mello   Layout: Jitendra Patil

DANGER IN THE PAST

Story And Script Prasad Iyer **Drawing** Archana Amberkar **Inking** Savio Mascarenhas **Colours** Umesh Sarode **Letters** Pranay Bendre

20

21

22

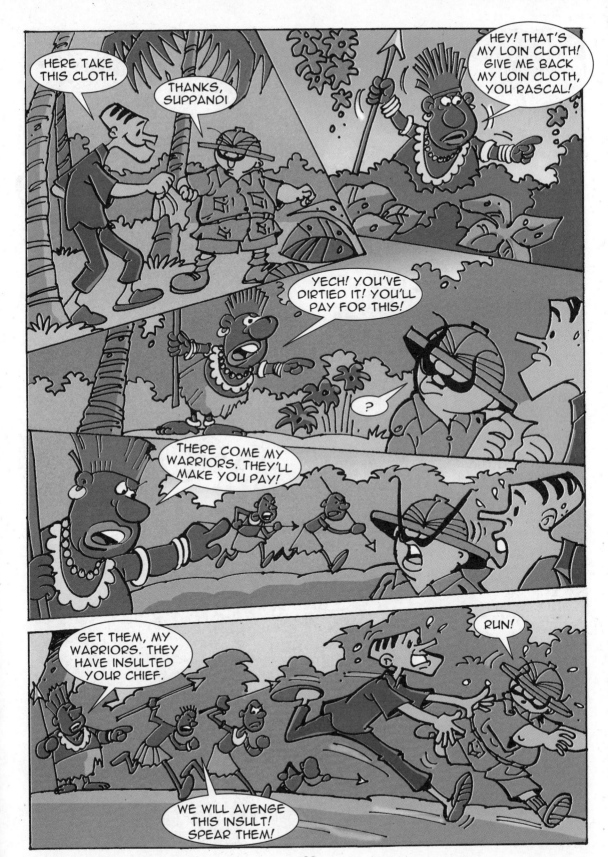

23

24

25

28

SUPPANDI AVATARS 1

Text: Sean D'mello   Illustrations: Archana Amberkar
Colours: Umesh Sarode   Layout: Jitendra Patil

SUPPANDI
Arts Of Living

Writer	Illustrator	Colourist	Letterer
Ashwini Falnikar	Archana Amberkar	Umesh Sarode	Prasad Sawant

30

31

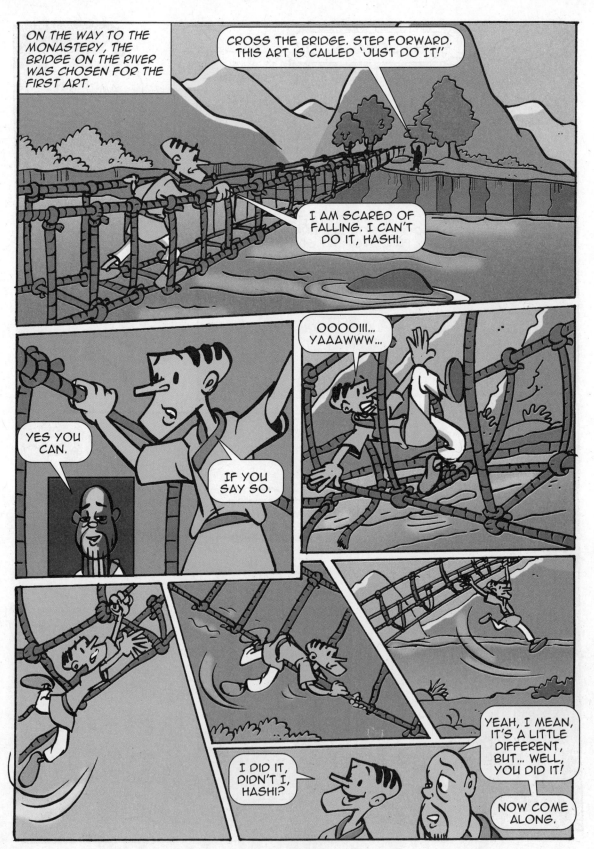

32

SPLASH

WHAT CAN I SAY? WELL DONE!

HUMM... HA...!

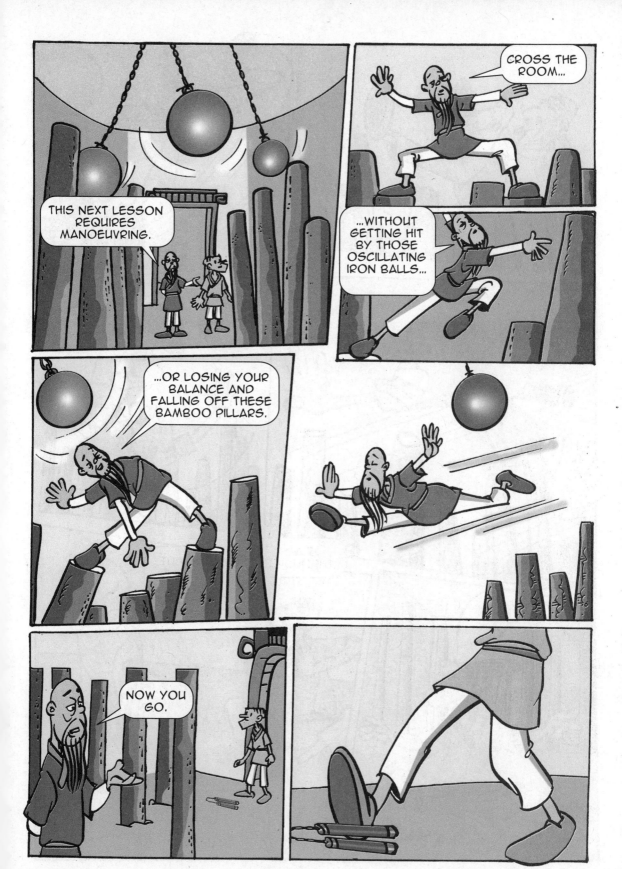

SUPPANDI EATS OUT!

Based on story by **Karthik Subramaniam**

Illustrator:
Archana Amberkar

Colourist: Umesh Sarode

38

SUPPANDI
Golden Rule

Story: Shivesh Shrivastava
Script: Rajani Thindiath
Art: Archana Amberkar

SUPPANDI GOT A LUCKY BREAK—HE WAS APPOINTED THE SUPERVISOR AT A FACTORY. ON HIS FIRST DAY —

SUPPANDI, THE GOLDEN RULE IN BUSINESS IS CUTTING COSTS! SAVE MONEY WHEREVER POSSIBLE! DON'T SPEND A PAISA MORE THAN NECESSARY. NOT A PAISA!

LEARN FROM ME! I ONLY FEED MY LABOURERS THE LEFT-OVER FOOD FROM MY RESTAURANT — I PAY NO WAGES! AND I ALWAYS GIVE MY FRIENDS A MISSED CALL AND WAIT FOR THEM TO CALL ME BACK!

I'LL REMEMBER THAT, SIR!

ONE DAY, THE FACTORY OWNER WENT OUT OF TOWN LEAVING SUPPANDI IN CHARGE —

REMEMBER MY GOLDEN RULE, SUPPANDI?

ABSOLUTELY, SIR!

WHEN THE FACTORY OWNER CAME BACK —

WHAT'S THIS?! MY FACTORY HAS BURNED DOWN! I'M RUINED!

SUPPANDI, WHAT HAPPENED? DIDN'T YOU CALL THE FIRE BRIGADE?

OF COURSE, SIR!

I FOLLOWED YOUR GOLDEN RULE AND SAVED MONEY. I GAVE THEM MANY MISSED CALLS - BUT THEY DIDN'T CALL ME BACK!

THUD!

Things That Happened in 1983

Hello, readers!
Do you know I was first conceived in the year 1983? Now 1983 was a long time ago, so it got me thinking, what other major events took place in that year? Surely 1983 had to be a memorable year. I thought I'd share some of its events with you.

Sally Ride, an American astronaut, rode her way into space in 1983. What makes her accomplishment special is that Sally became the first American woman to go into space when she flew aboard the space shuttle Challenger on June 18, 1983. Sally also still remains the youngest astronaut to be launched into space. She was only 33 at the time of the launch. Maybe I should become an astronaut. My employers always tell me to 'aim for the stars'; this way I can finally achieve my a goal.

Speaking of the stars and the moon, 1983 was also the year that Michael Jackson, the great pop musician, first performed his famous 'Moon Walk'. I was very surprised when I read this because I was certain the first moonwalk was performed by Neil Armstrong in 1969. Anyway, this moonwalk soon became Jackson's signature move, and is now one of the best-known dance techniques in the world.

The moonwalk wasn't the only explosive thing to happen in 1983. On January 3, 1983, the volcano Kilauea in Hawaii began spewing lava. Kilauea hasn't stopped erupting since that time. This makes Kilauea the longest-lived rift-zone eruption* of the last two centuries. That's actually quite a coincidence because a lot of people around me have been exploding since 1983 as well.

*Rift zones are basically huge cracks in volcanic mountains. It is from these cracks that the volcano erupts and the lava flows out.

Text: Sean D'mello   Layout: Jitendra Patil

TINKLE

IN THE TINKLE UNIVERSE, ONE YEAR EQUALS FIFTEEN MONTHS!

PICK UP A TINKLE SUBSCRIPTION TODAY AND GET AN EXTRA 90 DAYS OF TINKLE FUN ABSOLUTELY FREE!

TINKLE MAGAZINE
ANNUAL SUBSCRIPTION
24 ISSUES OF TINKLE MAGAZINE
+ 3 ADDITIONAL
MONTHS FREE

GET 3 EXTRA MONTHS FREE

~~MRP ₹960~~
OFFER PRICE ₹849

GET 3 EXTRA MONTHS FREE

TINKLE COMBO
ANNUAL SUBSCRIPTION
24 ISSUES OF TINKLE MAGAZINE
+12 ISSUES OF TINKLE DIGEST
+ 3 ADDITIONAL
MONTHS FREE

~~MRP ₹1800~~
OFFER PRICE ₹1649

☐ PAY AN ADDITIONAL ₹300 TO RECEIVE COPIES BY COURIER
PLEASE ALLOW FOUR TO SIX WEEKS FOR YOUR SUBSCRIPTION TO BEGIN!

DISCLAIMER: The product images shown are indicative. Actual product...

YOUR DETAILS
Name: .... Date of Birth: ☐☐ ☐☐ ☐☐☐☐
Address: ....
City: .... State: .... Pincode: ☐☐☐☐☐☐
Phone / Mobile No.: ☐☐☐ ☐☐☐☐☐☐☐☐☐☐
Email: ....

Parent's Signature

PAYMENT OPTIONS
Cheque/DD: ☐☐☐☐☐☐ drawn in favour of 'ACK MEDIA DIRECT LTD.' on bank ....
.... for amount .... Dated: ☐☐ / ☐☐ / ☐☐

SEND US YOUR COMPLETED FORM WITH YOUR CHEQUE/DD AT:
ACK MEDIA DIRECT LTD, AFL HOUSE, 7TH FLOOR, LOK BHARATI COMPLEX, MAROL-MAROSHI ROAD, ANDHERI (EAST), MUMBAI 40...
CUSTOMER SERVICE HELPLINE: +91-22-49188881/2   E-MAIL: CUSTOMERSERVICE@ACK-MEDIA.COM

YOU CAN ALSO LOG ON TO WWW.AMARCHITRAKATHA.COM TO SUBSCRIBE ONLINE!

47

SUPPANDI

A Confectionery

Story:
Shivesh Srivastava

Script:
Ashwini Falnikar

Illustrator:
Archana Amberkar

Colourist:
Umesh Sarode

*A dairy product

...AND SUPPANDI PACKED SOME SWEETS FOR THE CUSTOMER.

AND THE CONFECTIONER NEVER SOLD INFERIOR SWEETS AGAIN!

SUPPANDI FUN FACTS

The world we live in is both weird and wonderful. You must be wondering just why I've now come to this realization? You see, my newest employer is the editor of several encyclopaedias. He hired to me to collect information about all things weird, quirky and bizarre. So I thought I'd take a break from all the research and share with you some of those facts.

● Did you know that a crocodile can't stick out its tongue? The crocodile's tongue is attached to the bottom of its mouth by a membrane. Poor Doob Doob, even if he gets the better of Chamataka, he will never be able to show it.

● The highest score ever recorded in a football game was 149-0. You're probably

wondering how a soccer team could be so bad that they let 149 goals be scored by their opponents. The truth is they didn't let in so many goals—they scored those goals in their own net because they were angry. A refereeing decision went against them in the game, and gave the opposition team a one-goal lead. Angered, they decided to spend the rest of the game scoring goals into their own net… 148 goals to be precise.

● The national anthem of Greece has 158 verses, which officially makes it the longest national anthem in the world, by length of text. The Greek national anthem is better known as the *Hymn to Freedom*, or the *Hymn to Liberty*. It was written by a poet named Dionysios Solomos. Solomos wrote this entire poem in a single month. To this day, there is no one who has managed to memorize the entire national anthem. You know what I find funny? It'll probably take longer for someone to recite the entire poem, than it did for Solomos to compose it.

Text: Sean D'mello   Layout: Jitendra Patil

SUPPANDI
Great Deal

Story: Neeraj M. Mehra
Script: Rajani Thindiath
Art: Archana Amberkar

SUPPANDI, BUY SIX PACKETS OF CHOCOLATE BISCUITS. MY FRIEND SHYAM LOVES THEM AND HE'S COMING TO TEA.

HERE, TAKE THIS 1,000-RUPEE NOTE. I DON'T HAVE CHANGE.

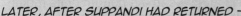

LATER, AFTER SUPPANDI HAD RETURNED —

SIR, THE BISCUITS AND THE CHANGE!

TEN RUPEES!

BUT EACH BISCUIT PACKET COSTS ONLY RS.10! SO THE SIX PACKETS SHOULD HAVE COST YOU RS.60! YOU SHOULD HAVE GOT RS.940 BACK!

THE CHOCOLATE BISCUITS WERE NOT AVAILABLE, SIR. BUT THEY WERE GIVING THEM AWAY FREE...

FREE!

...WITH A CAN OF OLIVE OIL WORTH RS.165. SO I BOUGHT SIX CANS OF OLIVE OIL, WORTH RS.990 AND GOT SIX PACKETS OF CHOCOLATE BISCUITS FREE!

WASN'T THAT A GREAT DEAL, SIR?

THUD!

SIR!!

52

SUPPANDI
in
TERROR MOUNTAIN

Writer: Prasad Iyer
Illustrator: Archana Amberkar
Colourist: Umesh Sarode
Letterer: Prasad Sawant

SUPPANDI'S NEW EMPLOYER WAS A MOUNTAINEER –

I'M GLAD I HIRED SUPPANDI AS A PORTER. SO MANY PEOPLE ADVISED ME AGAINST HIRING HIM...

...BUT THEY'RE ABSOLUTE FOOLS BECAUSE HE IS A FIRST-RATE CLIMBER – AND HE'S CARRYING THE LOAD OF THREE MEN, FOR THE PRICE OF ONE.... HEE HEE!

SUDDENLY –

OOPS! I'VE LOST MY GRIP!

PHEW! GOT IT!

SUPPANDI DOES AS HE IS TOLD...

...BUT, UNFORTUNATELY, IN ORDER TO UNBUCKLE HIS BELT, HE HAS TO LET GO OF THE CLIFF.

WHAA...

WHEW! WHAT A DREAM! I'M GLAD IT WASN'T FOR REAL. MY FRIENDS WERE RIGHT... SUPPANDI COULD BE THE DEATH OF ME!

SIR, YOU ARE AWAKE! GOOD! I'VE PACKED OUR KIT. WE ARE GOING TO CLIMB MOUNT ROCKFACE, AREN'T WE?

YOU...YOU... **GET OUT!** YOU'RE FIRED! DO YOU UNDERSTAND? SACKED!

EH?

I NEVER WANT TO SEE YOU AGAIN! SHOO!

WHAT DID I DO? WHY WAS I SACKED? IS THERE NO JUSTICE IN THIS WORLD?

POOR SUPPANDI. HE WASN'T AWARE, BUT HIS REPUTATION HAD CAUGHT UP WITH HIM.

SUPPANDI

shopping for chittu

Writer:
Dolly Pahlajani
Illustrator:
Archana Amberkar
Colourist:
Umesh Sarode
Letterer:
Pranay Bendre

SUPPANDI OFTEN ACCOMPANIED HIS EMPLOYER'S WIFE AND HER DOG ON EVENING STROLLS. ON ONE SUCH EVENING —

TEMP

CHITTU, NO! HELP ME RESTRAIN HIM, SUPPANDI!

YAP! YAP!

I THINK CHITTU LIKES THAT BALL...

YES... BUT, THAT SHOP IS TERRIBLY EXPENSIVE!

TEMPTING TOYS

PUSH

WOOF!

WE'LL BUY HIM A BALL FROM THE CHHOTA BAZAAR FLEA MARKET. IT'S NICE AND CHEAP. LET'S GO.

OKAY, MA'AM.

TEM

SUPPANDI! WHY ARE YOU GOING IN THE WRONG DIRECTION? THE BAZAAR IS THIS WAY.

ACTUALLY MA'AM, I'M GOING TO DROP CHITTU HOME FIRST.

WHY?

WE'RE GOING TO A FLEA MARKET. I WOULDN'T WANT CHITTU TO BE INFESTED, WOULD I?

SUPPANDI AVATARS 2

Text: Sean D'mello   Illustrations: Archana Amberkar
Colours: Umesh Sarode   Layout: Jitendra Patil

SUPPANDI
KEEPING WARM

Reader's Choice: Anindita Bhuyan, Assam

Script Sean D'mello   **Pencils & Inks** Archana Amberkar   **Colours** Umesh Sarode   **Letters** Pranay Bendre

SUPPANDI, I'M GOING FOR A JOG. FETCH ME MY GLOVES FROM THE CUPBOARD.

WHAT DO YOU NEED YOUR GLOVES FOR, SIR?

THEY'LL HELP KEEP MY HANDS WARM IN THE COLD.

THAT NIGHT, AT THE DINNER TABLE—

SURELY, YOU'RE NOT GOING TO EAT WITH THOSE DIRTY HANDS?

SHOULDN'T YOU WASH THEM?

ER... YES, SIR.

THE WASH BASIN IS RIGHT THERE... WHERE ARE YOU GOING?

I'M GOING TO FETCH MY GLOVES.

GLOVES? WHY DO YOU NEED GLOVES?

THE WATER IS TOO COLD, SIR. THE GLOVES WILL HELP KEEP MY HANDS WARM.

65

SUPPANDI
Spreading Christmas Cheer

Story	Script	Pencils & Inks	Colours	Letters
Savio, Rajani & Dolly	Dolly Pahlajani	Archana Amberkar	Umesh Sarode	Pranay Bendre

CHRISTMAS EVE NIGHT... IT WAS CLOSING TIME FOR 'BUY OUR DESIGN', THE BIGGEST DEPARTMENTAL STORE IN TOWN. AND THE TASK OF KEEPING IT SAFE RESTED WITH ITS NEW NIGHT GUARD, SUPPANDI.

HERE ARE THE STORE'S KEYS. AND THE CHRISTMAS CHARITY SACK FOR THE ORPHANAGE, SELECTED FROM OUR REJECT GOODS. SOMEONE WILL DROP IN SHORTLY TO PICK IT UP.

RIGHT, SIR. GOOD NIGHT. AND MERRY CHRISTMAS.

15 MINUTES INTO THE JOB...

(SIGH) I WISH I WERE OUT CELEBRATING WITH MADDY.

(YAWN) I WANT TO SPREAD SOME CHRISTMAS CHEER, NOT SIT IDLING HERE.

IT'S TIME TO ROB THIS STORE NOW. HOHO!

LOOK BEHIND YOU, SUPPANDI!

72